Anthony J. Drexel Biddle

The Flowers of Life

Anthony J. Drexel Biddle

The Flowers of Life

ISBN/EAN: 9783337055325

Printed in Europe, USA, Canada, Australia, Japan

Cover: Foto ©Andreas Hilbeck / pixelio.de

More available books at **www.hansebooks.com**

THE FLOWERS OF LIFE

BY

ANTHONY J. DREXEL BIDDLE

Author of "An Allegory and Three Essays."

PHILADELPHIA

DREXEL BIDDLE, PUBLISHER

WALNUT STREET

1897

To one whose influence, like some radiant star,
Brings Heaven's holy beauty from afar:
My life, my all—my Wife—to ever be
My guide throughout the long eternity.

Several of the writings in this collection are republished from periodicals and revised from a brochure entitled "An Allegory and Three Essays."

SUBJECTS.

The Flowers of Life

IT seems that there must be slothfulness among plants as among people. For of two plants of the same kind growing side by side, does not often one use its productive powers and cover its branches with floral beauty while the other remains flowerless?

We see two men: the one living for the pleasure and the betterment of his fellow-beings, and the other, like the flowerless plant, absorbing all the benefit he can derive in life, being too slothful to give forth or to develop in turn any beauty or good of himself.

We value a plant according to the delicacy and number of flowers it produces. And what joy flowers give! We remember them long after they are withered and dead.

This lesson then seems to be taught by the

flowering plants which give beauty to the earth and fragrance to the air:

To develop the good which we gather and to make it blossom into noble deeds.

And there is so much good to be gathered that if all men reproduced but a half of that they absorbed, it seems that this world would then become the flowering garden of Paradise.

A Forest Idyl

THE forest rustled:
   And sun-silvered leaves
Flashed merry sparkles
Through the shading trees.

The brooklet gurgled
O'er its pebbly bed,
Reflecting the sparkles
Anon, overhead.

Clouds above thickened
In gathering storm,
And hiding the sun
Made the wood forlorn.

Then bright lightning flashed
Most vividly bright,
And relit the dark
With great streaks of light.

15

But the lightning wild,
With its cold, fierce rays,
Set the wood groaning
And its trees ablaze.

The brook sighed : " Return
Sunshine, soft and warm !"
Gentle light sheds good,
Not lightning of storm.

Truth, Love and True Love

TRUTH lasts eternally; and God is love:
So love and truth are blessings from above.
If true love bind true lovers, God's image
Exists in them, in their earth's pilgrimage.

On the Death of the Only Child

THE summer's night was dark and still.

My wife and I sat in our little hovel. Our eyes were dry from long continued weeping, for the child, the only child was dead and gone!

We thought and wondered of the great unknown: was it life or death beyond the grave? We wondered. It had seemed with the birth of our child that our spirits joined for eternity. But now, in infancy, the child had been taken from us. What could be God's meaning?

We were poor, poverty stricken. But happy in each other, our happiness had been crowned complete when we felt our souls united in our own, our new-born babe.

Ah, how my Love did long to die! And naught but misery ahead in life I saw.

"My wife, my own!" I cried, "together let us yearn to see again our child. Together, with such strength of yearning, hope and faith that we *shall* see him."

How thus I spoke I do not know. But as I spoke my wife and I arose. Out into the night we stepped, and met a glorious vision. It was an angel, tall and fair and radiant, with sky-blue eyes and hair and wings of gold.

Upon our knees we fell.

The angel spoke:

" Your child has died to ye that ye may better live. His infant soul is of your spirits blended. Thus in him now ye have a heavenly place. But this remember well, small is his life. And if ye grow estranged his soul will die. So keep together in the desperate struggle, being always brave and of perfect comfort to each other. Life in your world is but your brief apprenticeship ere soaring unto greater things. Employ well your talents, for through your earthly workings *solely* do ye make yourselves of sufficient importance to exist eternally. Life beyond the grave means progression. And if together ye'd progress, united ye must be."

Lightning flashed from heaven, the spirit vanished, and again we were in darkness. But in the darkness we had seen the light. And through our sorrow we had seen eternity.

A Corporeal Argument

THE flesh and blood held argument.
Is not this passing strange,
That joint parts of the same body
Should each other derange?

Quoth blood, "I course the body through,
You, flesh, remain stock-still."
"'The stanchest is the truest," said
The flesh. "You do me ill."

Then up spake bones in lofty scorn:
"Why argue or dissemble?
'Tis I support you both," said bones;
And flesh and blood did tremble.

Ah, weak is flesh, and weak is blood,
And even bones decay!
'Tis the unseen, silent spirit
That ever wins for aye.

27

The Mountain Climber

A MAN set out to climb a mighty mountain in a day. He must race against time. He must concentrate his energy to a single end, and, once embarked upon his upward way, the greater efforts he put forth, the faster he would ascend. Stopping by the wayside, ever and anon, for refreshment and to indulge the pleasures of rest or of idle loitering, would deter his progress.

Like he who would achieve eminence in the limited period, his lifetime, the mountain climber should not tarry save for the necessary refreshment of rest, else, ere he knew it, darkness would have closed about him : like the laggard in life's climb whom death o'ertakes.

Hence onward and upward the traveller climbed. Sometimes he fain would stop to while the time or to find interest by the way-

31

side. For he thought to himself, at such periods, "Why should I reach the top to-day?" and again, "Of what benefit is it to me if I gain the summit at all?"

Here, in reply, a spirit voice advised: "Thou hast considered; thou hast chosen; thou hast set out to accomplish. Now neither turn back nor loiter. For, if thou doest *either*, it were better thou hadst not started to ascend."

Thus advised, the traveller hastened onward. For he felt that though he might fail to reach the summit ere darkness came, nevertheless a steady and unwavering tread would leave a distinct footprint in the pathway of example.

And thus, by dint of faith and perseverance, the traveller at last did reach the summit of the mountain, ere his sun had set. And here he needs should rest and look about him, for he now had well earned his rest and, having a better view than in the lowlands whence he came, he could put his power of sight to good advantage.

But alas, how few who thus gain the summits of their mountains *do* stop. They are now weary, but the fever of climbing is upon them.

The traveller saw a peak still higher than that upon which he was, and extending up into the heavens. Although his day was far spent, he again hurried upward.

In life's brief day is it meant that we should accomplish all things? Ere the traveller attained this greater height, the night had fallen.

Eternity Means Advancement

LOOK up into infinite space and be assured of the eternity of your soul. New stars are discovered constantly.

Eternity means advancement. To fill infinite space will take eternity.

We are God's servants. What does Christ's parable of the talents teach? To labor; not to idle. Why should we live eternally else to accomplish? Would a spirit exist without an object?

It is often queried, "What is the use of succeeding? Of what avail is getting ahead? There is nothing new to be accomplished: does not history repeat itself?"

Half of our people exist in a state of stagnation as much as possible. Many of the poor bemoan their fates, but do nothing of themselves to better their condition. Many rich retire from business to live on their incomes, and to dawdle their time.

The rich are rich that they may help their needy fellow-men to rise by proper uses of their talents and wealth. They are intended as the stepping-stones for the less fortunate across the river of trial to the shore of success.

Rich and poor alike who are idle cannot realize that true enjoyment is the reward of the industrious only.

Days of inactivity are the unhappy and discontented ones. We cannot successfully steal rest; we must earn it. And we must be honestly and healthfully weary to enjoy it.

The temporal system must be based on the eternal. To live properly here we must have occupation. In heaven it is surely intended that we have work to do!

But perfection is not to be looked for in this world. Can its attainment ever be expected in the next? Are not the countless, most distant interests of heaven and earth so closely related that to reach the verge of perfection in any one study is to cross the border into another, unlearned?

"NOTHING NEW UNDER THE SUN"?

The master labors; must not his servants labor?

If there has ever been something new to be done—and always will be—can the saying that "there is nothing new under the sun" hold good? If so, then surely, we can compile a catalogue of the world's doings and sayings during a certain given period which will be applicable as a reference for all time.

Calumny and treachery, disease and death have existed and will exist, but there are ever new forms in their perpetration and occurring. Choose one of these calamities at random, for illustration: disease. Why does a doctor, attending two persons of the same sex, like temperament, same age, and suffering from equally acute attacks of disease known by a single name, cure one patient and lose the other? Is it not because certain complications have arisen to change the unfortunate patient's disease into a *new* disease, unknown heretofore to the doctor?

Can you find two pansies alike?

New metals and new chemicals are being discovered and made constantly by combinations (heretofore unexperimented) of metals and chemicals already known. And here—

IMAGINATION IS THE CREATIVE POWER.

While imagination exists there will ever be new creations.

God imagines, and we are his creations.

IMAGINATION, THE MEANS TO COMPREHENSION; OR, IMAGINATION AS APPLIED TO THE OBJECT OF ONE'S INTEREST.

A man has a hobby. He believes in it. He pins his faith to it. He finds more interest incorporated in the subject of his liking than in all else in which he is not interested.

Then his imagination forms the magnifier through which he further pursues his study of this, his favorite object. And he quickly discovers that outside subjects are connected with his own so closely that, by a thorough mastery of his own subject, he learns a deal of others, *nolens volens.*

The history of the world may be traced in the life of an insect.

"Increase and multiply," is the Almighty's command.

Can even an insect find in death extinction of life, since there is unlimited space to be filled by new worlds to contain life?

No. At least no, if eternity means advancement; for then *no* life can be lost.

Remarks

THE end of this world will come when enough good souls have been furnished God's kingdom to meet His purpose concerning them.

We may write our lives illegible to man but not to God.

'Twere punishment less distressing to be in hell, forgotten to heaven, than in God's wastebasket of poorly-written lives.

If we lived life here a thousand years, we could not master temporal problems. Hence, how are our minds in their present state of being fitted to cope with questions of eternity?

Endurance is the proof of greatness. God lives eternally. And God watches over the life of an ant. He who best attends to the little things of life is foremost in the largest.

The only reliable implements for succeeding are wits well sharpened on the grindstone of work.

The ignorant may conquer, but only the wise can maintain mastery.

The stumbler upon success is more likely to fall than he who sees success before he reaches it. For successes in this world are the summits of the mountains of ambition, and prove dizzying heights for all but the very surefooted.

It is the hard things of life which soften the right nature while they strengthen the character.

An overdose of praise poisons rather than nourishes the successful.

An author must work with as fine care as a cutter of precious stones, if he would have his output possess the sparkle of a true literary gem.

Elegant paper and a tasty binding are as necessary to the serving of a good book as a clean and pretty dish is to the serving of a delicate sweetmeat.

The land of dreams is the borderland of reality.

Thought bounces at corners through the mind like the revolving ball on the billiard-table.

Negligence is the root of every evil.

Comparison with no other body of water can belittle the ocean's vastness; but the near-sighted often think the shallow pool profound.

He who for counsel depends upon others, stumbles blindly through life. Not a man's friends, but his conscience should be for him his judge and dictator. To lead a life of worth (and to be a leader of men), one must be an independent thinker.

In the earnestness of youth there's little faltering.

Be wary of him who is hard to offend.

Opposites are fitted for each other. In the one is what the other lacks.

The Book

HOW literature influences the lives of men! The reading of a great book furnishes the mind. The eating of nutritious food furnishes the body. But the mind is retentive, whereas the benefit of food can be only ephemeral.

Many men fashion their lives according to the teachings gathered from a single book. Self-made men, the most successful, serve as a constant illustration for this statement. It is rarely that a self-made man does not attribute his success to an early inspiration from some book. True, many self-made men are unlettered. But then it requires little schooling ere one of wit can understand the writings of the great. Wisest sayings are couched in simplest language.

Great books make great men.

Good literature is the rock whereon are the buildings of truth, wisdom, morality and heroism. So long as the rock holds firm, humanity's storms of doubt will not destroy its (the rock's) buildings.

The Newspaper

THE world could feel, the world could taste— but the world could not think, for it could not see, it could not hear, it could not speak. In the daily press the voice of the world has been found, and also the sight of the world and the hearing. Resultant is a power of universal thought in common : the gift of gifts to the human race. A universal civilization is made possible.

The great newspaper is imbued with an individuality more powerful than any one person can possess. It is an authority upon many subjects, whereas a great man is rarely an authority on more than a single subject. And even on this he cannot offstand the newspaper. It will win his knowledge, or he must *seek* its columns for the large audience he would obtain.

As for institutions, no other institution is so far-reaching, so penetrating, so influential. The great "daily" is at once an authority of the community in which it is published, a mouthpiece of the wise, and a chronicler of the world's history.

The reporters of a city are its discoverers. In bringing crime to light, detectives find it hard to compete with the news-gatherers; and in recognizing merit in worthy citizens of a community, the papers are invariably foremost.

A progressive, modern city is coming to be known by its leading papers, rather than by its prominent people. It is the press of a city that gives to it its individuality.

The power of a progressive nation is now reflected in its press. The more influential countries are those of the greater newspapers.

The press of a progressive nation may be likened to the stem of a tree, the people to the roots, and the government to the branches which the roots would have upheld. The stem is the means of conveying that nourishment from the roots *to* the branches which causes them (the branches) to grow ever stronger and more spreading. The doing away with the press of the progressive nation would affect that nation as the severing of its stem would affect the growing tree. Reasons might be summed :—

The stimulant of advancement is competition. The requirements of a competitive people, though unlimited, are met in their press, the scope of which is unlimited.

Mr. Harry Furniss, the distinguished English artist and caricaturist, said recently, on returning from the United States to his native land, "The key-note of America is competition; for instance, when I had arranged to join the New York *Herald*, I received a cablegram from another journal, 'We double the offer.' They did not in the least know what my terms were; but it was competition, and they were ready to fight."

The press is the only medium in which the ever-increasing demands of the public are satisfied. It is at once, then, the people's most popular and most powerful institution. They find in it all that is encouraging. It upholds them and their standards, and in doing this it upholds their government. And it keeps them and their government thoroughly informed as to each other. The government addresses its people through the newspaper column, and thus it makes known its demands and necessities. In turn, it looks to the press for information of its people.

The newspaper is read by every class and condition, from the lowest to the highest. Hence a needy case in any walk of life, when brought to notice through publication, finds sympathizers and helpers. The great newspaper has its columns ever open to the free use of the suffering and oppressed.

The journalist may arouse public indignation or enthusiasm as required, and the newspaper readers are an all-powerful society in common, ever ready to right wrong or to commend. Thus, in the truly great newspaper, neither the mighty nor the lowly are spared their deserts, be they blame or praise. So that neither evil nor good can escape publicity.

Books are a luxury that cannot always be enjoyed, but the modest price of a newspaper places it within reach of even the very poor. The newspaper critics have made a garden in the barren plain of necessity. They cultivate the finer plants of art, science, music and literature, and remove the weeds of ignorance detrimental to their growth. In the prominent newspaper is found the best of literature. Leading authors, appreciating a wide circulation, now like their works to appear in the press prior to publication in book form.

As the promoter of business and enterprise the newspaper stands alone. As an advertising medium it is unrivalled. The smallest schemes have developed into the largest through proper newspaper noticings and mentionings. And the successes of many great business establishments are reached chiefly through the judiciousness of their newspaper advertising.

The gatherer of thought, the journalist, should be well adapted for political life: he has opportunity to study disinterestedly the wants of his people before taking high political position. Journalism teaches loftier principles than ward-heeling. There are to-day some thirty-three newspaper men in our House of Representatives, and the British House of Commons contains about twenty-eight prominent journalists.

Mr. Furniss says, "America recognized that daily illustrated papers were to be part of the national life of the future, and it got the machinery ready. The daily paper rules in America, and it will rule in England."

The Mind

THE mind is the soul's machine. It is the mind through which the soul expresses itself and improves or deteriorates itself; the soul is the motive power, the mind the motor, and the body, the servant and physical supplier of the mind.

Knowledge is that which is gathered from the mind's working process, thought: it goes to build up the soul (knowledge, be it understood, here signifying the result of experienced living).

The mind gathers or photographs knowledge-pictures on its sensitive film, and presents these pictures to the soul; so the soul receives impressions and fashions itself accordingly.

As all things physical may be likened to one another, and as both mind and body are alike in that they are servants of the soul let us compare them.

There are different kinds of minds and there are different kinds of bodies, but all are machines.

Of course there are, and must be, many different kinds of machines in this go-ahead world; but the question arises, which are the most desirable and most successful?

Choose, for instance, between the machines of the professor and of the practical man, of the student and of the originator.

The question is sometimes asked, "Has the mind a limit?"

The answer to this must be simple, for all things physical have a limit, and the mind is physical.

Here we might observe, "there then must be such a thing as 'too much learning.'" And may it not be even thus?

Indeed it is thus: at least to the practical, advancing, originating mind. For in such a mind, where learning is of great assistance, too much learning, like water thrown on a fire, or like oil flooding a machine, stops the progress.

The mind of an originator, an author, an inventor, or of any progressive man might be compared to a slate. When it has been filled it must be emptied ere it can have other contents.

And, in the case of the mind, its contents, while fresh, should be put forth into a new idea, a new book, a new invention or a new composition.

It (this creative mind) is then ready to contain other knowledge which must never be so crowded as to prevent or restrict the working of thought, that process whereby old knowledge is revolved into new. Here, again, the creative mind might be likened to a churn into which is poured a fluid for the producing of a solid. If the churn is filled to overflowing it will not work properly.

Once more, by way of example, we may liken the mind to the body. When it (the mind) is overstacked with knowledge it seems to become like the over-muscled body of the strong man: lumbering, awkward and unfit for quick action. Contrast the all-round athlete with the so-called "strong man." Take for example the boxer and the weight-lifter; the boxer is not overburdened with heavy, cumbersome muscles, though he is strong and agile.

The weight-lifter is possessed of abnormal development which necessitates slow and restrained movements of the limbs, as over-developed muscles tend to bind the human body like tight cords—thus rendering agility, litheness of limb and suppleness out of the question.

Each of these men has good and bad points in his make-up; but pit the two against one another and which would win in an encounter? The boxer, nearly always.

A law-school graduate often does not know as much as his professor when he leaves college, though he may soon distance him in life's race.

His mind is not so full that he has no room left in it for original thought and energy.

Verily, while book-learning is desirable, the school of experience is a most excellent teacher.

Motive

THERE are two ways, at least, in which every idea may be expressed. Probably to no form of expression does this saying apply so forcibly as to the explaining of motive. Three-fourths of literature and two-thirds of conversation contain theory or motive. All that is written or spoken must be prompted by theory, motive or contemplation, else it is utterly useless and worthless to the reader or auditor.

Without the power of reason, little save vegetable life could exist. · The power of reason is the self-preserving characteristic in everything possessing animal life. In its primary form, among the lower orders of animals, it is known as instinct; and in its high form, among humankind, as intellect. Animals evince their possession of instinct by action, while human beings may show their powers of intellect by words (as well as by behavior).

All verbal or written expression must contain reason or motive to be of value. An author is prompted by motive when he takes up his pen; —every book written should set forth some elevating, instructive theory.

There are two styles of literature, viz.: moral and immoral; but the writers of the moral eclipse the writers of the immoral literature.

There are at least two ways in which the same idea may be expressed; and thus it is with the writers of moral literature. Some make their motives clear by narrative, wherein they lead their readers to obtain the best points of view unexpectedly, " by winding paths." Others address their readers directly, in discussions of the motive theories themselves. The former is the more general and popular style of literature, but it is a question whether the latter is not the more instructive and more practical.

Again, the practical argument has much more

weight with the average person than the religious. The way to reach the masses is through practical reasoning; when the writer has his readers thoroughly interested in his subject and has established a bond of sympathy between himself and them, then, and not till then, may he successfully introduce religious sentiment into his treatise.

Motive is the motor, and in another sense the key, to action.

Opinion

OPINION is the result of thought, and by opinion breadth and depth of mind are made known.

All minds run in grooves; narrow minds run in narrow grooves, and broad minds run in broad grooves.

A versatile mind is a broad mind: a mind which is sympathetic and which can adjust itself to the understanding of any other mind with which it may have to deal.

Be it understood, however, that it is not a changeable mind here meant, as such is again another type. No, a broad mind is more what might well be termed a graceful mind, which strongly holds to its own good opinions, unless it finds better. In which latter case, even though it make the discovery, as it does not infrequently, in an inferior mind—the latter being a specialist on some subject into which the broader mind has not had time to look—it may accept opinions of the inferior, and show its broadness in so doing.

A stubborn mind is a narrow mind, in that it will not listen to other opinions, but is always roused to anger when in debate or argument.

Righteous wrath is excellent. Narrow-minded wrath (the expression of envious hatred) is not only foolish but harmful, and full of evil, breeding wickedness; it should be crushed out and gotten rid of, for it spreads like contagious disease among neighboring narrow minds, and, if allowed to spread, creates a false state of affairs; this then can only be stopped with an outburst of indignation by all broad minds and true consciences united.

And here again opinion decides the turn, for the broad and deep minds send forth a flood of opinion that sweeps away the bravado and bitter opinion of the shallow minds.

" By their works ye shall know them," is Christ's teaching. Is not a man's opinion the key-note to his mind?

The Life of an Ephemeron

'TWAS the dawn of a summer morning. The moon, loosening the cable of silvery light which moored her to earth during night's brief season, was drifting into the obscurity of the heavens before the search-light of the rising sun.

From the eastern hemisphere, that seemed as a great sea of flame, came ripples of light earthwards through the heavy, hazy atmosphere; twilight turned swiftly to daylight.

Near the centre of a large, dismal swamp stood a cluster of stunted willows. Weeping indeed they seemed, for the gloominess of their situation was sufficient cause for such emotion. A solitary crow, perched among the topmost branches of one of the trees, intruded an occasional croak upon the death-stillness of the marsh. A poisonous snake, gliding beneath the tree in which the mournful bird was ensconsed, lifted its

---

NOTE.—Ephemeron, derived from the Greek ἐφήμερος, is a species of butterfly which lives but one day.

head, cast a glassy stare upwards, and then disappeared in some rushes which grew close by.

Upon the tree hung a number of chrysalides, and from them white-winged butterflies began to flutter forth.

The crow, thereupon, spread his wings and hopped from the branch upon which he had so long been perched. Flitting about the tree, he caught many of the tiny ephemera as quickly as they flew from their birthplaces. Few escaped the lightning beak of the cruel bird. Those that did, made their way through the air to a neighboring tree and there rested a long time. They were bewildered and dazed.

The sun rose ever higher in the cloudless heavens, and the tiny butterflies at length took not heart, but wings, and flew away in a cluster altogether.

The sun's rays drew a damp vapor from the swamp, and the tiny travellers found it difficult to make headway. Many rests were taken, for their wings became heavy with the moisture in the air.

Still they instinctively struggled forward in the direction of the mainland. They seemed set upon the idea that once there, they should be happy and free from all danger.

They still remained together, for "misery loves company," and, like all things in nature, the butterflies had no desire to be alone until they were well situated.

Suddenly, as they were flitting over some tall, wavy grass, something arose and flew toward them. They remembered the black-winged monster that had devoured so many of their companions, and they flapped the air convulsively in their fright.

Just before the plover (for such it was) had reached them, an explosion was heard, and the butterflies' pursuer fell to the ground.

The little group hurried onward in silent wonderment, and a few minutes later passed an immense giant, holding a smoking stick in his hand. Just then a bee joined the butterflies; he told them the shortest way out of the marsh, and, moreover, said that what they had just passed was a man, their preserver, who had slain the bird with a gun which he carried. The bee had scarcely finished speaking when a swarm of mosquitoes came by; some were puffed out and reeling through the air, while others buzzed discontentedly. The bee said they were pursuing the man.

"Their sole pleasure in life consists in bleeding people and becoming intoxicated therefrom," continued the bee. "They have no occupation, and consequently spend their existence in dissipation; they get no real enjoyment out of life, as they do not appreciate or understand it. They die young, and the world is glad to get rid of them."

The butterflies' eyes were being opened.

From the tall grass arose a large creature with magnificent wings; it sailed grandly along, a little in advance of the butterflies. Many of the latter were lost in admiration, for it appeared evident that the one in advance was of their own species. A few of the butterflies stayed independently behind, while the majority hastened forward and joined the newcomer. The latter accosted the little innocents pleasantly, and conversed so glibly and entertainingly that they became spellbound with delight.

They had not seen sufficient of the world as yet to be able to distinguish a moth-miller from a butterfly; it was not long before the creature with the beautiful wings had quite gotten the tiny flutterflies into his power. Away he flew, back to the recesses of the swamp, and they innocently followed him. Only one succeeded in separating himself from the misguided group.

He had a long and painful journey before he caught up with his wiser companions; for they had flown straight ahead, and were now far in advance.

When he finally reached them they were resting on a tree at the edge of the great swamp. They seemed to have entirely forgotten their companions who were led astray, for, when the belated butterfly fluttered up and lit on a twig close by, they were chatting gayly and looking out into the bright world which lay before them. They were glad to see their old companion, however, and greeted him cordially. He told them how their comrades had been taken back to the vile marshes by the superb-looking creature which they had mistaken for a butterfly; he had discovered it to be a pretender. He said the creature's wings had been only gilded, and the beautiful tints were wearing off, even before he had taken his departure. When the butterfly had concluded narrating his experience, it was unanimously agreed that it was not wise to put faith in new friends until their wings had been thoroughly tested.

The butterflies remained on the inner edge of the

swamp for a long time. There seemed to be a certain morbid fascination for them in looking back into the dismal marshes and reviewing the past.

At last, the experienced butterfly (for we shall call him this hereafter, in order to distinguish him from the others) aroused his companions.

"Come, let us fly forth into the bright sunshine of life," he said.

The others arose therewith, and they all flew from the swamp in a solid cluster.

They intended always to keep together, but they soon found that this was impossible.

They had gone but a little distance before one of their number fluttered blindly into a spider's web, and became so entangled therein that the rest were obliged to leave him to his fate and fly onwards.

Shortly afterwards, while passing a large bonfire which burned on the outskirts of a forest, another butterfly, becoming fascinated by the fire's brilliance, ventured too near, and was licked in by the flame.

The rest still pushed ahead, and entered the wooded expanse by a straight and narrow road leading through to open fields beyond. Many alluring paths diverged to the right and to the left, however, and the butterflies soon began to take to these in preference to the straight, uninteresting road. All that took them wandered for awhile and became lost eventually in the depths of the forest.

At length, when the end of the narrow road had been reached, the experienced butterfly was the last of all the companions that remained. When he flew out into the fields beyond the wood, he was the only one that, born in low surroundings and wishing to soar above them, had finally attained his object.

And now the sun had reached its meridian, and the ephemeron's life was half spent. The tiny traveller was unconscious of this fact, nevertheless, for nothing in nature knows the time when it will cease to exist.

There was a large daisy field near by; the butterfly flitted in to sip the fragrance from the flowers. As he alighted upon a poppy he heard the sound of voices close by; he crawled to the edge of the flower, and looking over discovered two ants on the stem of the plant, directly below him.

Seated together in the shade cast by the flower, they were holding a spirited discussion; the subject of argument was whether the spider or the bee possessed the more industrious and enterprising disposition.

The ephemeron played eavesdropper, and this is what he overheard:

First ant:—"The spider has no enterprise!"

Second ant:—" How so, dear aunt ?"

First ant:—"The spider labors with but one object in view, that of securing his own personal comfort. When he has built a domain for himself, he retires from active life and is content for the rest of his existence to live in idleness and seclusion."

Second ant :—" For that matter, then, the bee has no enterprise."

First ant:—" Here, again, you are mistaken, aunt." (Among the ants there is but one relationship.) "The bee labors also, but not only for the betterment of her own condition, but for the betterment of the condition of the entire community in which she lives as well. When she has filled her treasuries with honey, does she stop? No, she builds other hives or treasuries, and proceeds to fill those likewise. She asserts her rights when it is necessary, and she takes the aggressive very quickly, too, when there is cause to do so."

A queen bee that had been sitting close by, unobserved by the ants, had listened to the entire conversation.

Having heard the many flattering compliments paid her, she arose majestically and flew off, feeling puffed up and proud beyond expression. It seemed to her that there was no one like herself. She felt that she was unapproachable, and that all the eyes of the world were centered upon her.

She was hovering over an ants' nest when a discontented darning-needle flew along.

He was "darning" everybody and everything, and he "darned" the queen bee as he passed her.

This was more than the latter's pride could endure, and she called after the needle to return at his peril. He no sooner heard the challenge than he wheeled about. A terrific combat was the result.

At last the grumbling darning-needle and the proud bee came tumbling to the ground together.

They fell, wounded and faint, upon the ants' nest. The many inhabitants came pouring forth and fell upon the unfortunate combatants. The ant upon the stem of the poppy, that had but a short time before been so loud in the praises of the bee, turned to her companion with the remark : " Even the mighty sometimes fall."

" Everything comes to him who waits," replied the second ant, referring to her spider theory.

The two then descended to the ground and joined their companions in picking the fallen bee and darning-needle to pieces.

The shadows had begun to lengthen when the ephemeron flew out from the daisy field. Finding a pretty country road, he flitted along and saw many novel and interesting sights ; there is always something new to be seen in life. The sun sank below the western hills, and the butterfly flew on through the increasing darkness.

At last he could go no further, so, fluttering to the ground, he sought a sheltered spot beneath some withered leaves; from thence he looked out into the blackness of the night. He was happy, very happy; he thought of the pleasant life he had had by keeping to the right roads. He looked back upon the past with contentment and satisfaction.

The drunken bats began to fly about, and the discontented owls hooted forth their complaints from a neighboring wood.

The cheerful crickets, on the other hand, chirruped forth in immense choruses, and the tiny ephemeron moralized that "the world was not so wicked, after all."

And now the butterfly's life was spent. He fell back and gazed upward at the stars; they appeared to be coming towards him, and to be twinkling all about him. (They were merely the fireflies which he saw.)

Suddenly the twinkling seemed to him to cease, and to appear as a great mass of flame.

Then all was dark: the tiny butterfly lay dead among the withered leaves.

THE MADEIRA ISLANDS,

BY

A. J. DREXEL BIDDLE,

Fellow of the American Geographical Society.

Containing twenty-seven full-page illustrations, a map of Funchal, a map of the Island of Madeira, showing districts devoted to vine culture, and a chapter of useful information for the traveler and visitor. 12mo., cloth, pp. 115. Price, $2.00.

What Leading Critics Say of this Work:

From the American Press.

"A very interesting book entitled 'The Madeira Islands' has been written by Anthony J. Drexel Biddle. . . . As for the text, suffice it to say that the author tells all that is worth knowing about the islands. He has evidently studied them and their history thoroughly, going back to the time when they were discovered and settled, and telling us how they have fared from that time until now. Of life in the islands at present he draws a graphic and interesting picture, and altogether his book can be recommended, not only to historical students and to those who may intend to visit the Madeiras, but also to those who, though unable for various reasons to spend much time in traveling, are yet always eager to obtain new information about foreign and little-known countries."—*The New York Herald.*

"Mr Biddle has the quick, observant eye of one who travels for the love of seeing strange sights. He has, moreover, a keen sense of humor, and the power to seize upon what is odd and picturesque."—*Brooklyn Eagle.*

The above work is for sale by all booksellers, or will be sent by Drexel Biddle, Publisher, postage prepaid, to any part of the United States, Canada, Great Britain, or Mexico, on receipt of the price.

" . . . Mr. Biddle's book begets a desire to visit the islands and see with one's own eyes what he has so graphically described; but whether the reader can go or not, he will be richly repaid for the reading of one of the choicest books of the year."—*The North American.*

"'The Madeira Islands' is in great demand."—*Ev'ry Month.*

" Mr. Biddle in this his latest contribution to literature has found the fortunate middle ground between a mere guide-book and an elaborate and technical record of the resources, population and general statistics of these beautiful islands. He writes vividly and with much keen observation of the climate and scenery, with picturesque descriptions of the fêtes, customs and manners of the native Madeirans. . . ."—*The Public Ledger, Philadelphia.*

" Books on these islands are rare, and none has shown such careful research and clever observation, combined with the short story-teller's instinct to ferret out a romance."—*The Critic.*

" It has been left to Mr. Biddle to be the historian of what under the magic of his pen are veritable 'summer isles of Eden.' And the spell of romance that the ill-fated history of Robert à Machin and his luckless love Anna d'Arfet casts over the beautiful 'Ilha da Madeira' seems to linger to this day."—*Seattle Post-Intelligencer.*

" . . . This account is anything but dry and perfunctory. It begins with a love story lived so long ago that it has become history."—*New York Recorder.*

" Entitled to be classed among the successful books of the current year."—*Book News.*

"'The Madeira Islands' is the name of a new book by Anthony J. Drexel Biddle. . . . The work is handsomely illustrated, and the reading matter will interest seafaring people as well as civilians."—*American Shipbuilder.*

" Contains much valuable information."—*New York Press.*

" Mr. Biddle has found in the Madeira Islands a fresh field in which to exercise his descriptive powers. . . ."—*Review of Reviews.*

" . . . Whether it is the blueness of the sea that he dwells upon, the mildness of the climate, the luxuriant growth of fruit and flower, the quaint customs of the Madeirans, or a gorgeous ceremony witnessed from the balcony of the Cathedral, his style is always fresh, vivid and instinct with the deep enjoyment of life. . . . There is so much in it, however, that is good, that it is difficult to make a choice."—*The Evening Item, Philadelphia.*

The above work is for sale by all booksellers, or will be sent by Drexel Biddle, Publisher, postage prepaid, to any part of the United States, Canada, Great Britain, or Mexico, on receipt of the price.

" It is one of those delightful volumes of descriptive writing that soon find a place in the hearts of the people."—*Sioux City Journal.*

" . . . The Islands have never been written up in attractive manner, and it was a very bright idea on the part of Mr. Biddle to take the work, which he has done uncommonly well. It is beautifully illustrated, and gives the facts of their history in a bright and very entertaining way, combining the dry with romance in such a manner as to hold the reader to the end. The life in the present is delightfully pictured, and the beautiful illustrations contribute to the charm. It is uncommonly well done, and the author, who has already won laurels as a writer of short stories, has rendered a valuable service to history."—*The Morning Telegraph, New London, Conn.*

" The pages are embellished with amusing anecdotes."—*Baltimore World.*

" There is not an uninteresting page."—*The Helena Independent.*

" The reading world will welcome this latest book of Anthony J. Drexel Biddle, because it has learned that in whatever he puts forth there is strength of thought, the result of labor and research, clothed in a lingual dress which adds to its attractiveness. This new book will increase his reputation as a ready and skillful writer, and as a man of great observation as well as reflective capacity. The author presents, in a series of eight chapters, all the facts of note concerning the island group, their characteristics, their products and commerce, and their population and history, and many of these are graphically illustrated with engravings. distributed through the book, which, once for all, can be recommended to the student of history, to the lover of good literature, and to the traveler who desires to fortify himself with information concerning a strange land he proposes to visit."—*The Brooklyn Citizen.*

" . . . Nearly ready, a new edition of the recent work, ' The Madeira Islands,' by Anthony J. Drexel Biddle. The author has made an exhaustive study of the Madeiras."—*The New York Times.*

From the British Press.

" One hears a good deal of Madeira wine—not so much, perhaps, as we used to do—and not a little of casual calls by pilgrims in quest of health ; but how little do we know of the Island itself! It has been left for an American to give us the first illustrated book on ' The Madeira Islands.' The author is Mr. Anthony J. Drexel Biddle, who has already made considerable contributions to contemporary literature. Mr. Biddle gives much most interesting information, and presents it in a very readable style, about Madeira. . . . Mr. Biddle presents a very useful book in ' The Madeira Islands,' interesting in its historical gleanings, and of practical value in the advice and hints it affords for all who think of visiting the Island, which is regarded by thousands of all nations as the Invalids' Paradise."—*The Sheffield Telegraph.*

"An enthusiastic account of the Madeira Islands."—*Manchester Guardian.*

"' The Madeira Islands' is a well-written volume, containing historical facts and pleasant descriptions of the Islands and the people who inhabit them. The author is evidently acquainted fully with his subject."—*The Birmingham Daily Gazette.*

"The author has already won his spurs in literature—in fact, the present work made its appearance in first edition form last year, and gained golden opinions. He is an apt descriptive writer and a clever story-teller. . . . The papers are all interesting, and they contain a great deal of useful information respecting things in general about the islands, their scope ranging from statistics about the population and items of legal interest to the gay and happy lives passed by the inhabitants, the flora and fauna, and the beautiful gardens, ' ribeiros,' and residences of Funchal. . . ."—*The London Transport.*

"This is a carefully-written historical and descriptive account of the Madeira Islands. . . . A picturesque account is given of the discovery of the first of these islands, on All Saints' Day of the year 1418. The rise and progress of the wine industry is traced, and many interesting facts given. The concluding chapter is full of useful information for the traveler and visitor. Routes to Madeira from the various ports of the world are tersely summarized. Practical information is given on the hotel service, private housekeeping, the servant question, and marketing. The book is entertaining and practically useful."—*The Sheffield and Rotherham Independent.*

" . . . Increasing as Madeira is every year in popularity as a health resort, Mr. Biddle's exhaustive account of the Island will doubtless find many appreciative readers."—*The Newcastle Leader.*

" . . . General knowledge of the Madeiras is, to say the least, but limited. Mr. Biddle, who is believed to be the first American who has penned a history of the Islands, is to be congratulated on the fact that he has succeeded in bringing within small compass all that is worth knowing of them. He draws a graphic picture of the life that may be spent there, and has much to say that will commend the happy isles to those who can afford a vacation in this charming resort."—*The Western Daily Mercury, Plymouth.*

The above work is for sale by all booksellers, or will be sent by Drexel Biddle, Publisher, postage prepaid, to any part of the United States, Canada, Great Britain, or Mexico, on receipt of the price.

From the Canadian Press.

" . . . Contains ample information, conveyed in a direct and simple manner, about the Madeira Islands, where Mr. Biddle resided for a year, devoting his whole time to collecting data for his valuable guide-book. It is the first illustrated work on the islands that has ever been published, and the author has endeavored to tell us in the compass of a hundred and eleven pages all that is worth knowing about their former history and present condition. . . ."—*The Montreal Star.*

" We heartily recommend it."—*Canadian Bookseller.*

"In these very disagreeable and trying months those who may be thinking of a finer climate and a change of scene will be interested in . . . 'The Madeira Islands.' . . . Part history, part guide-book, part purely descriptive and literary. There are also maps and plans, lists of steamer communications, with prices and all needful information for travelers. The historical part is very useful and convenient, all available sources having been tapped by the author. . . . It is therefore possible to have a perfect rest from riddles of existence and problems of politics and questions of literature in that delightful land of forgetfulness and silence amid the ever-shining seas."—*The Mail and Empire, Toronto.*

From the Scottish Press.

" The author of this interesting and prettily illustrated hand-book summarizes the present situation at Madeira thus. . . ."—*The Scottish Geographical Magazine.*

" . . . There is certainly more life in it than is usually found in a guide-book. If its style and tone are essentially American, the volume is not unentertaining, as well as useful. . . ."—*The Edinburgh Scotsman.*

" Consists of a number of detached papers, of which the common feature is that they are readable, and that they contain a great deal of information, both interesting and practically useful, about the Madeira Islands. . . ."—*The Glasgow Herald.*

The above work is for sale by all booksellers, or will be sent by Drexel Biddle, Publisher, postage prepaid, to any part of the United States, Canada, Great Britain, or Mexico, on receipt of the price.

THE

FROGGY FAIRY BOOK.

Popular Edition. Duodecimo, 66 pp., fully illustrated, printed from original plates, in green art vellum binding, and stamped in red and gold and red and silver. Price, 50 cents.

FOR A CHRISTMAS, NEW YEAR, EASTER OR BIRTHDAY GIFT.

Edition de Luxe, limited to eight hundred copies, printed on extra heavy, super-calendered paper, with nine full-page illustrations such as every child will love; bound in red and gold, gold edges. Price, $1.25.

Of this edition the Augusta, Georgia, *Herald* says : "Taking into consideration the heavy satin-finished paper and the exquisite illustrations, it is one of the handsomest books for children that has ever come to this department."

The above work is for sale by all booksellers, or will be sent by Drexel Biddle, Publisher, postage prepaid, to any part of the United States, Canada, Great Britain, or Mexico, on receipt of the price.

PRESS COMMENTS.

"Frogs in literature are associated in most minds with fairyland. No one is surprised at any adventures froggy may meet with, after the fate that befell 'The frog that would a-wooing go,' so many years ago. One of the best successors of that ancient idyl that I have seen for years is 'The Froggy Fairy Book,' written by Anthony J. Drexel Biddle and illustrated by John R. Skeen. It tells of how little Elsie met a funny froggy, who came to her in evening dress, with a lantern in his hand and a violin under his arm. After that there is a frog orchestra, a frog prince, fairies of all kinds and plenty of fun. It is a real old-fashioned tale, told with the sympathy of one who loves children and knows how to write for them. The illustrations are excellent. The type and paper are good and the volume is handsomely bound."—*New York Commercial Advertiser.*

"The Christmas books of Mr. Anthony Joseph Drexel Biddle, the American writer and publisher, are becoming increasingly popular."—*London Literary World.*

"Mr. Drexel Biddle, of Philadelphia, has published a new edition of 'The Froggy Fairy Book,' by Anthony J. Drexel Biddle. The binding and the illustrations, which are by Mr. John R. Skeen, might almost suffice to account for the remarkable popularity of the little volume. On the other hand, however, it must be admitted that without either of these adjuncts the mere text would have been quite deserving of the favor to which three editions in less than six months abundantly testify. Taking it altogether, the book is the very thing to delight children."—*Glasgow Herald.*

The above work is for sale by all booksellers, or will be sent by Drexel Biddle, Publisher, postage prepaid, to any part of the United States, Canada, Great Britian, or Mexico, on receipt of the price.

" . . . Remarkably clever, and the long-haired young lady who has wandered into Frogland is charmingly contrasted with frogs, who figure as portly elderly gentlemen, or are got up like respectable family butlers."—*The London Times.*

"This little fairy-story gives an apt illustration of the difference between the American and the English child. . . ."—*The Spectator, London.*

"Elsie Lee is as American as 'Alice in Wonderland' is English. It is a pretty and healthy story, which is certain to delight all good children."—*The Scotsman, Edinburgh.*

" . . . Parents at their wits' end for a new sensation to keep the little folks quiet, even for a time, will welcome the second edition of 'The Froggy Fairy Book,' by Anthony J. Drexel Biddle, which has just come from America. It is unnecessary to explain the 'plot' of this most entertaining fairy tale. Suffice it to say that it contains all the elements of wonder required to gain for it the approbation of the children, while the excellent pictures are in themselves an exhaustless source of interest."—*The Dundee Advertiser.*

"It will hold the young mind."—*Cork (Ireland) Examiner.*

"It is full of childish interest."—*The Canadian Bookseller.*

"A funny book for children, which has obtained a great vogue."—*Pall Mall Gazette.*

"The story, which is cleverly conceived, tells of the adventures of Elsie Lee, a typical little American girl of tender years, among the frogs that inhabit a certain little brook near Elsie's home. . . . Superbly bound. . . . A leading feature of the work is the illustrations, drawn by the well-known artist, John R. Skeen, of the Philadelphia *Times*."—*The New York World.*

"Fairy-book literature receives an accession in A. J. Drexel Biddle's 'Froggy Fairy Book.'"—*Boston Globe.*

" . . . Every parent will be happy to see the pretty book in the hands of every child."—*Chicago Times-Herald.*

"The story has hit the popular fancy."—*Brooklyn Standard Union.*

"The publisher has given us a handsome piece of bookmaking in this unique work. . . . Wide-awake children will give it a hearty welcome at any season of the year. The author has followed out a queer conception, and has done it in such a pleasing manner as to assure his place among the successful writers of fairy literature."—*Good Housekeeping.*

The above work is for sale by all booksellers, or will be sent by Drexel Biddle, Publisher, postage prepaid, to any part of the United States, Canada, Great Britain, or Mexico, on receipt of the price.

"'The Froggy Fairy Book' will be received with transports by the juvenile world of readers."—*The North American.*

"One of the successes of the season."—*The Philadelphia Times.*

"Sure to amuse the children."—*San Francisco Call.*

". . . Worthy of special mention as illustrative of the imaginative faculty of the writer, controlled by consideration for the capacity of those he writes for. The language of the narrative is from 'the well of pure English undefiled,' and almost all the words used are monosyllabic, and so adapted to the understanding of the child who reads or only listens; and all who do will surely call for the second 'Froggy Fairy Book,' which is promised from his pen."—*The Brooklyn Citizen.*

"'The Froggy Fairy Book,' by Anthony J. Drexel Biddle, though of the holiday order, is a book for all seasons. It will never come amiss in any child's library. It is ingenuous, quaint, full of strange conceits and always interesting. . . . Children of all ages will find delight in its pages."—*The Budget.*

"The author of this work is Mr. Anthony J. Drexel Biddle, a young American journalist, who has already made his mark in literature. A simple, old-fashioned fairy tale, it treats, as its title indicates, of some adventures in Frog-land. Elsie Lee is a typical little American child. . . . As may be imagined, she has plenty of fun, and all this is interestingly described for the benefit of young readers. . . . The book is in every way calculated to please the little folk for whom it is intended, and by whom a much better present could scarcely be desired."—*The Western Daily Mercury, Plymouth, England.*

The above work is for sale by all booksellers, or will be sent by Drexel Biddle, Publisher, postage prepaid, to any part of the United States, Canada, Great Britain, or Mexico, on receipt of the price.

SHANTYTOWN SKETCHES,

A Collection of Short Tales in Irish, Negro and German Dialects,

BY

A. J. D. B.

Paper, 12mo., pp. 72.   Price, 35 cents.
The above work is for sale by all booksellers, or will be sent by Drexel Biddle, Publisher, postage prepaid, to any part of the United States, Canada, Great Britain, or Mexico, on receipt of the price.

SOON TO APPEAR.

BY THE SAME AUTHOR.

WORD FOR WORD
AND
LETTER FOR LETTER,

A NOVEL.

A New, Enlarged and thoroughly Revised Edition of

THE MADEIRA ISLANDS,

Containing nearly fifty full-page illustrations and numerous maps, together with additional chapters on the History, the Vine, the Wine, and the Flora.

www.ingramcontent.com/pod-product-compliance
Lightning Source LLC
Chambersburg PA
CBHW020034030726
47499CB00007B/2422

* 9 7 8 3 3 3 7 0 5 5 3 2 5 *